Poetry Playground

DARREN CARTER

To order additional copies of this book, contact:
Xlibris
0800-056-3182
www.xlibrispublishing.co.uk
Orders@ Xlibrispublishing.co.uk

Contents

Oak Tree

I am a wise old oak tree.
I stand in a meadow by the sea.
I can tell you tales of what I have seen.
History come and gone.
Battles lost and won.
Young love,
Holding hands under my tree.
When they kissed,
It was nice to see.

The birds of the air,
Take their shelter in my wooden hair.
My leaves,
Keep them dry,
From the rain drops from the sky.

I had a conversation once with a Magpie.
There was only one,
Which made me cry.

The farmer ploughs his field,
So the humans can have their fill.
Every season comes and goes.
Farmer Giles plants and sows.
He takes his break up against the trunk of my tree.
He eats his sandwiches and drinks his tea.

It is now time for me to take my sleep.
I am so tired, but I need to speak.
Watch over me while I dream,
Of a fairy tale by a stream.
But one wish I will ask.
Don't let the humans use their axe.

Rainbow

I am a rainbow.
I only know to be sad.
I have been like this ever since the world was first bad.

I was created out of love.
Because my Creator hurt the world from above.

Man can be so bad.
I come out because God is still mad.

I may have a Pot of Gold.
But it still makes my heart of my rainbow so cold.

When the world is good.
I am not seen.
When the thunder and lightning strike.
I come out to make things right.

All the colours of my rainbow,
Are there to make everyone aware.
That thunder and lightning can strike anywhere.

Mr White

Hello,
I am Mr White blood cell.
I am here to make you well.
Germs look on me as a bit of a bully.
All I do is keep this body running smoothly.

I do my job,
Day and night.
When you get the flue.
I am called upon to fight.

I don't get much time for a hobby.
All I do is keep this body healthy.

It would be nice to have a girlfriend.
But then I would have to pretend.
That I am something better.
As the girls like a cell who has a lot to offer.

My story ends,
When my shift comes to a close.
When this body begins to decompose.
I don't get a pat on the back
Or a watch and chain.
All I get is a rotten corpse in a grave.

Frog

I am a frog.
I sit on a lily pad in the valley.

All I do is get up and eat my food.
Then I go to sleep and dream what I would like to do.

Would I need an education?
To get ahead in the world of mechanisation.

Would I study cooking.
I better not as I may end up in the boiling.

I have always liked the idea of being a scientist.
But someone might come along and give my neck a twist.
I think I am bright.
My father told me that last night.
I better study medicine.
But I may end up as a specimen.

I could become a photographer.
But the model may eat me with a cauliflower.

Actually,
The world doesn't offer me anything.
I rather sit here and think of nothing.

The Change

A lonely caterpillar on a leaf.
Keeping an eye on the enemy in the sky.
Knowing they would rather see him die.

The change begins to happen.
He is worried with the reaction.
He is beginning to feel sleepy.
Now he is away from the enemy.

He breaks away,
Full of colour.
A butterfly ready to flutter.

His wings ready to fly.
A Red Admiral in the sky.

Wise Owl

Wise owl in the tree,
Are you hooting at me?
Tell me what you know.
Do you know how flowers grow?

Why do you look like you do?
Is it because Nature loves you.

Do you know how to solve equations?
Can you make sense of my tribulations?

I would love to take you to school tomorrow.
But if you flew away,
It would bring me so much sorrow.

I could try and come this time again.
But my Mother won't let me,
Because it's passed my bedtime.

Good night wise owl.
Don't hoot to loud.
I need my sleep.
I have a busy week.

Little Notes

Little notes on a bar.
You make such beautiful music for the size you are.

You are all stars in your own right.
The instruments play you with such delight.

I will now play your tune.
I will always thank you.
For bringing music to my ears.
It is a melody I will always want to hear.

Bumble Bee

The bumble bee flies alone.
He makes the honey when he gets back home.

Every flower he visits.
He takes the pollen like a Mexican bandit.

In the hive,
The bumble bee makes the honey sweet.
The children love it on the bread they eat.

When you see the honey jar.
Wherever you are.
Always think of the busy bumble bee.
He made the honey for you and me.

Home Sweet Home

Home sweet home is where the heart lives.
Your mother tucks you in and gives you a bedtime kiss.

At Christmas time,
The family cheer,
Looking out for Santa Claus,
When he comes this time of year.

The home is where,
We come back to at the end of a busy day.
When we are tired and travelled a long way.

In our beds warm and tight.
The house keeps us safe during the night.

Gold Fish

A gold fish in a bowl.
Swimming around,
With nowhere else to go.

He made a wish.
He would like another fish.
He would like a mate
They could go on a date.

This made him very happy.
He swam around the bowl,
Even more quickly.

His wish came true.
Now there are two gold fishes in a bowl,
Swimming around with nowhere else to go.

Balloon

Flying in a balloon.
Looking down from a sky so blue.
Looking at life carrying on.
As I listen to radio one.

They look like ants running about.
Driving their cars around roundabouts.
Flying over the patchwork of gold and green.
Drifting along in a summer so serene.

Seeing the top of the trees.
I think I am going to sneeze.
I think my hay fever is here.
It's making my eyes run with tears.

I see the birds flying high.
They are now saying their goodbyes.
My time has been well spent.
It is time for me to descend.
All good things come to an end.
Tomorrow I will fly at half past ten.

Christmas Tree

Christmas tree,
Christmas tree,
What presents have you got for me.
Different shapes,
Different sizes,
All lovely gifts to make the children excited.

The fairy lights,
What a beautiful sight.
Like the star of David on the nativity night.

The baubles,
To fend off the evil eye.
To keep children safe
And keep their parents in smiles.

The star at the top of the tree.
Marks the beginning of the nativity.

The Christmas tinsel of colours so bright.
Fills the children with delight.

Tick Tock

Tick, tock.
Tick, tock.
Is the sound of the Grandfather clock.

A Grandfather of time.
Stands proud and tall.
It's pendulum swings to and thro.

The hands are going around.
The time is nearly found.
The clock is about to chime.
The hour is here.
We know the time.

Bird of Fire

Bird of fire.
Renewed by the flame.
The Ancients loved her.
Phoenix was her name.

Rising from the ashes.
No need for three wishes.
The Phoenix takes flight and kisses the wind.
A bird with golden wings.

City of Troy,
A far of land.
Saw the beauty of the Phoenix over the desert sands.
Majestic and free.
Like a child of Nature should be.

Precious to the myth of Nature.
A kindred creature.

Nature's Dream

A maiden so pure and meek.
On her bed of roses deep.
A sleeping beauty that never sleeps.
Watches over those in her keep.

Mother Nature lies alone.
A statue hewn from oak, Beach and Elm.
Dressed in ages of the past.
As timeless as an hourglass.

A fruitful vine around her waist.
On her head a crown of grace.

The coolness of the midnight air.
Casts reflections on her face so fair.

Blessings come,
A new day brings.
The dawn has awakened,
The colours sing.

When dawn comes,
The windswept curtain falls.
Brings forth,
The new eternal dew,
To cherish the old and bless the new.
The symphony of the birds,
A chorus of the season they are greeting.
The melody of the whispering wind,
lies gently on the crest of their wings.

Under the vastness of heavens wake.
Of thunder and lightning make.
The tear drops of the living water flow,
Nature's children drink down below.

When the storm breaks the calm,
The warmth of the sun the bringer of its charm.
As heaven sent,
A gift from above.
The hues of the rainbow,
Promised in love.

Valkyries of the Storm

Valkyries of the storm.
Riders of war.
Where there is honour.
Let there be our reward.

Beautiful warriors of the axe.
Let it be ours we ask.
Take us now to Odin our lord.
So we can be forever mourned.

Let the arrows of fire.
Light up our warrior desire and take us to Valhalla,
A place of honour and valour.

Sun Rise

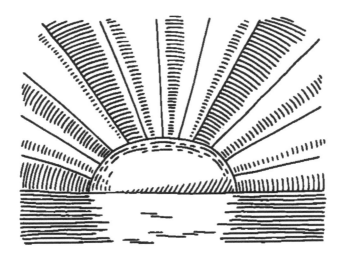

Let the sun rise,
Into the heavenly skies.
The angel's praise the summer haze.
The start of a new day,
Brings happiness in every way.

Looking forward to what the new day may bring.
The angel's in heaven watch and sing.
They wish the world to have good things.
So they will always honour the King of Kings.

Merlin of the Cave

Merlin of magic.
Merlin the wise.
The stars of the heavens reveal your surprise.

In a puff of smoke.
The magic words you spoke.
Are as old as time.
You speak them always in rhyme.

"That Arthur is King and Lord of all.
His kingdom will never fall.
Excalibur is his alone.
He is King and Lord for whom I atone.

He will be betrayed by friendship and love.
A victim of the blessed blood.
He will shed a tear in secret.
His love will long for worship.
A Knight of nobility.
Will be cast away and live with his blame every day.

I am Merlin of the cave.
What I see, will be.
I can't turn back the tide.
Time will run.
Time won't hide.

His kingdom will lie in ruin.
He will always damn a woman.
Forever he will wish he never met a Knight.
He will forever wish he never gazed upon his sight.

His name is Sir Lancelot of the Glen.
Arthur will never speak of his name again."

Octopus

I am an octopus.
I have tentacles.
The only problem is that I can't see without my spectacles.

The other octopus' laugh at me.
Because without my spectacles,
I can't see.

I am also a vegetarian.
The octopus' think I am an alien.

Sometimes,
I wish that I was a shark.
At least then,
The others would be hiding in the dark.

Triangle

I am a triangle.
I am in love with a square.
The only problem is that he acts like I am not there.

I try and make him aware that I exist.
But he thinks I have gone around the twist.

He thinks I should find myself another triangle.
But I like squares,
Because they have four right angles.

Hot Chocolate

At night I turn off the light.
I need your warmth tonight.
Dark and creamy.
You are so dreamy.
Sweet on the tongue.
Sweet to the taste.
Not a drop goes to waste.

You help me to sleep.
I need my beauty sleep.
You will help me dream the night away.
So when tomorrow comes.
I am ready for the new day.

Wishing Well

Wishing well.
Wishing well.
Throw a coin in my well.

Make a wish,
You wish to make.
Close your eyes and wish with all your strength.

Make a wish,
Be a star.
What magical wonders lie too far.

They may be hidden or in the open.
They may come with love.
Spoken with words from the Lord above.

Oh, Teddy Bear

Oh, teddy bear.
I love you most dear.
When you get upset.
I wipe away your tear.

Oh, teddy bear,
With an ear torn away.
You will never leave me.
You will always be my friend every day.

Oh, teddy bear,
At bed time,
You are always there.
When I wake,
I kiss you,
Because of your sad stare.

I promise oh, teddy bear.
When I have my own daughter.
I promise you oh, teddy bear.
She will love you like no other.

Sunflowers

Reaching out to catch the suns warmth.
The sunflowers sway in the summer months.

In a golden meadow,
Filled with golden romance.
The sunflowers with happiness shall dance.

As Nature showers them with her loving promise.
Immortalised by a man's sadness.

Easter Bunny

The Easter bunny is at play.
You only see her on Easter day.

She runs around the countryside,
With her sisters.
When Easter time ends,
They disappear.

They leave behind an Easter to remember.
So children will always know of,
the sacrifice of the Saviour.

Land of Make Believe

To dream beautiful dreams,
While I sleep.
Is a pleasure I will keep.

The secrets I dream,
Are only for me.
They are a fantasy only I can see.

In my dreams of dreams.
I can be anything I wish to be.
The land of make believe,
Is just for me.

So take me there.
I wish to dream.
I wish to be in a state of grace and dream of a heavenly place.

Eagle in the Sky

Into the desert I will fly.
An eagle in the sky.
I have freedom of will.
I can see the evil of men still.

My domain is the sky.
I am alive.
I can feel the breeze of the Creator.
I can feel the love of Nature.

Fly away.
I will fly.
I am an eagle in the sky.

Magic Carpet

Across the skies of the desert of hidden eyes.
Towards the horizon of the sunset, rise.

Magic carpet,
Take me to the winds of my dreams.
Take me where I wish to go.
Take me where the Devil dares not to follow.
Take me towards,
The lovers light.
Take me there,
I wish to love the night.

Sacred Wish

The sky of delight.
Make your wish tonight.
I am,
the Genie of the sacred wish.
What you ask of me,
I shall give.

Wealth, fame or power.
Your wish is my desire.

Oh master,
I will grant your wish of wishes.
You will receive all your riches.

So rub my lamp.
It will shake and rattle.
Then I,
The Genie of the east,
Will finally be released.

The Eskimo and the Polar Bear

A lonely Eskimo in an igloo.
He was very hungry,
So he went to the pool.

The Eskimo sat on the snow to fish and waited for the fish to bite.
A Polar Bear crept up on him and gave him a fright.

The Polar Bear fancied the Eskimo to eat.
But the Eskimo suffered with sweaty feet.

The Eskimo was very brainy.
He convinced the Polar Bear that he was to bony.

So the Polar Bear sat by the Eskimo,
Waiting for the fish to bite.
They waited all night.

When morning came.
No fish were caught.
The Eskimo was sleepy.
The Polar Bear was still hungry.

The Eskimo went back to his igloo to sleep.
The Polar Bear followed his food to eat.

Sweet Echo

Sweet echo,
Where do you go,
When you leave my lips.
Who will kiss me when I speak.

Where does the breeze take you?
Where does it leave you?

Sweet echo,
Never go.
I like the sound you make.
You could make the mountains shake.

Tell me now,
Sweet echo.
Where do you go.
As when silence comes,
I miss you so.

Take me with you,
Sweet echo.
I want to go.
I will follow you wherever you go.

Tell me where you go,
Sweet echo.
I will never tell a living soul.
Because I love you so.

Beauty

Beauty,
Oh beauty.
You have a holy duty.
To speak without words.
No lies are heard.

Truth,
Is there for all to see.
Truth,
Is there for others to try to be.

The truth is without disguise.
It comes from one with love in their eyes.

Hercules

The Lion of Nemema.
With club, bow and arrow ready.
Hercules did battle against his first enemy.
Every thrust of his metal,
The creature prevailed.
Hercules killed the creature.
He skinned the beast of Nemema and used his skin as a form of armour.

To the swamps of Lerna,
Hercules went.
To kill a giant Serpent.
Eight heads turned to two.
When one was cut off another one grew.
One was immortal,
Not like the others.
Hercules used its blood on his arrows.

Hercules had now to bring back to Eurystheus the Great Boar.
He chased after it till it couldn't run any more.
He stayed with the Centaurs.
But one was under the spell of sacred wine.
The others attacked in great numbers.

Hercules fired a rally of his deadly arrows.

Hercules again was set a trial by Eurystheus.
Ravenous birds from the Lake Stynphalus.
Athena instructed Hercules to put the two bronze plates together.
This would shield him from their metal like feathers.
The birds flew out from their hiding place in great numbers.
Hercules killed them with his poison tipped arrows.

Next was to clean the Aegean Stable in one day.
This was easy for Hercules,
As he was a son of Zeus any way.
He broke down the wall,
Built a canal and diverted two rivers.
To satisfy the disbelievers.
The water came and made it clean.
It also cultivated the land and made it green.

Breakfast at 8

Sitting around the kitchen table.
With the tea pot with the chipped handle.
The toast,
Nice and warm.
Standing to attention in the rack.
Waiting for the impending attack.

Butter ready to be spread.
The children love it on their bread.
Boiled eggs waiting to be cracked.
Tea spoons in hand ready to smack.

The toasted soldiers gathered for their duty.
They are dipped and swallowed readily.
Butter and marmalade on the toast.
The children love this time the most.

Licking of lips.
Sticky finger tips.
Finishing my cup of tea.
Then it's washing up time for me.

Wild Horses

Wild and free.
Wild horses.
Pure as Nature.
Sons and daughters of Pegasus.
With souls of greatness.

One became a Greek victory.
Many lives were lost to this horse of history.
Whispering to the sun.
As free as Natures children.
As free as the wind.
Children of the storm.
Their spirit will be forever their own.

Santa on strike

The news flash of the year.
Santa Claus is on strike.
As no one has showed Christmas cheer and he needs to rest his reindeer.

The world looks within and blames each other for the mess they find themselves in.

Parents are sad for the children,
With their sad eyes.
The whole universe can hear the children's cries.

The fathers are in distress,
Because Santa has caused a mess.
What can the world do?
To change Santa's bad attitude.

All the leaders of the world,
Go to make Santa understand.
That he has made all the parents very mad.

All Santa wants is a helper.
As he is getting a lot older.
He will place an advert in every newspaper.
So he can bring back the Christmas cheer.

Mouse Trap

A mouse trap placed on the floor.
Waiting for the last piece of the jigsaw.
A piece of Cheddar.
So the mouse can meet its maker.

"Don't these humans know," says the mouse in his hole.
"Mice don't eat cheese because it makes us sneeze."

Old Windmill

Old windmill on the hill.
With white roses by your windowsill.
Who waters them so.
They are as beautiful as the Winter snow.

Old windmill on the hill.
I like to play by you during the day.
Because on the Summers day,
You keep the heat of the sun away.

Old windmill on the hill.
All you do all day is make that rickety sound.
I like it,
As it always lets me know you are around.

Travellers Prayer

Travellers pray to Saint Christopher this day.
So your journey will have no danger,
I pray.

He will keep you safe,
On your journey so long.
He will make sure you are safe,
Till you arrive back home.

Say a prayer of thanksgiving to him.
For making your journey safe from dangers so unforgiving.
He will cry in your praise.
He will always watch over you in every one of your days.

Homework

It's that time again,
Homework.
I rather be watching television.
But I need to do my revision.

I will start with equations.
They make me scratch my head.
I have to remember what my teacher said.

I am so confused.
I will never get this right.
I will be up all night.

I have other subjects to do,
Like English, French and Chemistry.
I can hear my mother in the kitchen washing my sports laundry.

I wish I had a robot.
I could ask him to do this for me.
He could even make me a cup of tea.

I could watch television.
While my robot works out this damn equation.

Mr Scarecrow

Mr Scarecrow,
Your clothes are worn and torn.
Your face looks all forlorn.
You scare away the crows,
Because you frighten them so.

You protect the crops and the seeds,
From these flying thieves.
You never move.

You never grow old.
You just stand in the field all alone.

Do you get lonely standing there?
Do the birds of the air play around with your straw hair.

I like you Mr Scarecrow.
You are a good listener and a good friend.
You will do your job till the bitter end.

Symbols

I am a fraction.
Some say I am an attraction.
I come into my own,
When your mother cuts your birthday cake at home.

I am an attention seeker.
I always want to know the answer.

I am the addition.
Some say I have an addiction.
I am used all the time.
I am in a state.
It always begins when the humans wake.

I am the division.
Some say I have lost my vision.
I wish I was something else.
I enjoy being by myself.

I am the subtraction.
Some say I am a bit of a distraction.
I like taking away.

It makes me very happy in every way.
Your lost is my gain.
I love it when humans use me again.

I am the equal sign.
I am the one at the end of the line.
I am more important than them,
As I tell the answer.
Which makes me in a way their leader.

The sum has no answer without me.
I bring mathematical harmony.
I bring all the numbers and symbols together.
The mathematical world feels a lot better.

Writing Bug

I have the writing bug.
Oh dear,
I have just spilt my mug.
I will have to start again.
As my coffee has stained.

But worst still.
My ink has run.
All the words I have just written have all gone.

What a wasteful day.
I will have to rewrite it all over again.
I wish I had a computer.
My life would be a lot easier.

I wouldn't have all this paper lying around.
If there was a fire,
They would be all lost and never found.

I must get myself a lap top.
Then I will be like everyone else.
I would have more time for myself.
But for the moment,
I will write with ink.
I now need to think.
Now,
What did I write.
It must feel right.
I love writing poetry.
It feels my life with beauty.

Book Worms

I am a book worm.
I am not a vegetarian nor a meat eater.
But I do enjoy eating the pages from an encyclopaedia.

Wherever there are books.
I will be there.
I am quite shy and small.
You will never know that I am around.
Till you open up a book and I fall to the ground.

I love eating a page.
I wonder if it will go with sage.
I haven't ever tried it before.
There may be a cookery book with a recipe for four.

My family are also here.
We are all from the same family tree.
We always stick together.
As a family of book worms,
are always stronger,
when they eat the pages from a novel of Harry Potter.

Leonard the Lemming

I am Leonard the lemming.
I am frightened by everything.
But when myself destruction calls,
And I need to go.
I can't.
As I suffer from vertigo.

The other lemmings jump off the ledge.
I can't even get to the edge.
I am so scared.
I run around instead.

I wish I was a Lion.
Then I would be strong and brave.
But I still wouldn't want to go to an early grave.

I could even be a bird.
I could fly away and return at the end of the day.
I wonder if birds suffer with my complaint.
As it makes me want to faint.

So before I die.
I will write a note.
To tell others of my predicament.

"Goodbye world.
I have to go.
When I jump,
I will keep my eyes closed."

Little Miss Ladybird

Little miss ladybird.
You always got your head inside a book.
What are the beautiful words you are reading.
Why aren't you outside flying.

Mummy,
I find that boring.
I rather be inside reading.
I love reading books.
I feel I would like to be a writer.
I can be something better.

But you are a ladybird.
That is what you are.
It is a honour to look like you do.
So always have a smile and go and fly for a while.

Fly with your friends on this Summer's day.
Your books will always be here,
When you return.
So enjoy your day and fly away.

Rag Doll Molly

Rag doll Molly.
I love you so truly.
I take you everywhere.
I hold you tight,
When I go up the stairs at night.

My mother,
Puts you inside my bed with me.
You always make me so happy.

My mother,
Kisses me good night.
Then she switches off the light.

I say good night to you and give you a kiss on your cheek.
I would love it so much if you could speak.

So I will say a prayer before I go to sleep.
To ask God for you to speak.

But if it doesn't happen,
Rag doll Molly.
I will always love you.
So don't worry.

Bullied

I am bullied at school.
I don't tell my mother,
Because the bullies will bully me further.

I don't like going to school.
I wish I was at home.
Then the bullies will leave me alone.

I wish I was a Super Hero.
Then I would be liked.
Everyone would be amazed at what I could do.
Then perhaps,
The bullies would leave my school.

My Little Shadow

My little shadow.
You are always there,
On the ground.
So please shadow,
always stick around.

When I sleep,
What do you do shadow?
Do you think about tomorrow?
Do you dream shadow?
Do you dream of a summer meadow?

My little shadow.
You are my silent,
Good friend.
You will always be with me till my end.

Toy Soldiers

In the toy box,
The toy soldiers lay,
Ready for the children to play.

Ready to stand to attention.
The toy soldiers are ready for the children's imagination.

Enter the world of fantasy,
The children go.
The toy soldiers will lead them to a place of perfect joy.

Moon

Let the moon shine.
Let its mystery take you to the Divine.

The crescent moon,
in the midnight sky.
Brings you joy,
In front of your eyes.

To shed a tear for the moon.
Cry to her and she will to.

The stars keep her company in the midnight sky.
They know of her loneliness and they keep her from her cries.

Crystal Ball

Oh, crystal ball.
What do you wish to show me this day?

You are the doorway to man's future.
Release your secret,
Let me see.
I wish to know what fortune lies in front of me.

A fairy tale,
Or a whisper of the past.
You are the key,
Which holds every secret which is cast!

Delve deep.
In the depths of the endless stream of knowing.
You will show me the truth by the morning.

Flight of Icarus

Fly, with angel wings.
To the celestial sky.
With a touch of humanity,
Takes me upon a wing of a heavenly humility.

The heat of the sun.
Shows the love that has begun.
Taken upon a prayer.
I will surrender,
To the heat of the eternal stare.

To enter the realm where angels dwell.
I taste the freedom of the air.
It is only for the God's to share.

I fall to the depths.
I have lived for this.
A moment of freedom.
I am the prisoner,
To the coldness of Poseidon's kingdom.

Father Time

Father Time.
A bearded man,
With angel wings.
Dressed in a robe of glory and light.
Carrying your scythe,
Your hourglass.
Which holds man's secret before his eyes.

Holding the hourglass of man's mystery.
You know the hour of it all.
You are the silence,
Which keeps it hidden from the world.

A vision of destiny and immortality.
The sphere of time.
The flow of the stream.
Time will remain,
For mortals to see.

The final end,
Is what we must all take.
It will allow time to finally have its rest.

Sand Castles

Imagine the dream.
Enter the world within.
Escape beyond heaven.
When the tide of the sea,
Takes away the mystery.

Sand castles,
of enjoyment and of joy.
Happier times,
When I was a boy.

Lost in time.
The memory of it is mine.
Let it come when I dream.
When I am old.
Let it take away the sadness of my world.

Piggy Bank

Piggy bank,
Piggy bank.
You are a lot cuter than a bank.
With your little eyes.
Looking so surprised.

Your little face.
Your little snout.
Keeping watch.
Making sure no robbers are about.

I can sleep happy in my bed at night.
Knowing my coins are safe and sound.
Till I wish to buy a toy from the town.

Jigsaw

In a box,
A jigsaw is ready.
For the child to take a journey of discovery.

For the puzzle to be solved,
A picture is given.
For the child to know,
When it is nearing completion.

Then the realisation appears.
As the picture is on the point to be revealed.

When the final piece of the jigsaw is placed.
A feeling of success and a smile appears on the child's face.

Sleepy Head

Sleepy head,
I think it is time for us to go to bed.

My eyes are heavy.
I feel so sleepy.
I need to go to bed,
Then I can go to sleep and rest my head.

Oh, what a yawn.
It will soon be dawn.
I need to go to sleep.
I can't get to my feet.

I think I will sleep on the sofa tonight.
I will wrap the throw over round me nice and tight.

Good Omen

Two beautiful angels escaped from heaven.
They took the opportunity when it was given.

Peter left the gate wide open.
These two beautiful angels took this as a good omen.

Now they walk the earth.
They have heavenly wealth.
Goodness of heart,
Souls of perfect light and a beauty which lights up the world day and night.

Derek

I am Derek the ant.
I have lost my pants.
I have looked in the wardrobe and under the stairs.
I can't find them anywhere.

I wish I could remember where I saw them last.
Because now I feel a cold draft.

I wish I had a better memory.
Is my name Henry.

I keep on forgetting what I was going to do next.
Which tie was I going to use around my neck.

By the time I remember.
I would forget it again.

I wish I could remember.
Blast!
It's gone again.

Sea Shells

The sea shell,
Holds the sound of the sea.
When you place it on your ear;
It plays the seas sweet melody.

The sound it leaves.
Is Poseidon's hello.
His daughters leave them on the shore,
For children to enjoy.

From the sea,
Beautiful eyes wait for the children.
When they come,
The Mermaids look on them as gifts from heaven.

The world is so beautiful.
Always let the children look on it as magical.

The Round Table

A blessed oak,
Was chosen for the Kings oath.

A table of the Divine.
A traitor would still reside.
But it was from the weakness of the flesh.
The Eve's curse showed its beautiful face.

Men of honour.
Sat around this table of King Arthur.
Their honour would live forever.
But one weakened at the final hour.

Swords of valour.
Would be laid upon this table of power.
Men of nobility,
Sat around this blessed table of Nature and divinity.

Mr Snowman

Mr Snowman made of snow.
I can see you from my bedroom window.
You stand so still,
Do you feel the Winter chill?

As the coldness of Winter remains.
Mr Snowman you will never melt away.
You are my friend,
In these cold days ahead.

You have a black hat upon your head.
You have a scarf around your neck.
You are happy in the snow.
What will happen when it goes.

I see you are melting away.
I will say my goodbyes,
Till Winter comes another day.

Sad Sofa

I am a sad sofa.
No one loves me.
I feel my time has come.
The family don't sit on me when they get back home.

I was used by the family when they needed a nap.
They had to be quick,
To beat the family cat.

I don't want to go.
I am happy in their home.
But they have bought a new sofa.
So it's time for me to move over.

Whispering Woods

Entering a new world of magical beauty.
A time lost to the whole of humanity.

A secret place,
Where Nature herself resides.
All her beautiful daughters are by her side.

The whispering woods,
Of forgotten dreams.
This fairy tale begins,
Without a kiss from a handsome prince.

Love and goodness are found here.
Their spirit remains throughout the seasons of the year.

When the sun rises from its slumber.
The trees protect this blessed place,
From God's angry thunder.

Nature begins this sacred story.
Her daughters begin their happy duty.

To bring enchantment and eternal blessing.
The birds of the air mark their beginning.

Mr Pumpkin Head

I am Mr Pumpkin Head.
I am bored.
I am waiting for Halloween to come around once more.

I am Mr Pumpkin.
I have evil within.
I see the world at Halloween,
As it really is.
Witches flying in the sky
And Ghost and Phantoms floating about.

The evil eye,
I can see.
When we meet.
It is a Halloween treat.

But now Halloween is over.
I am taken away from the window.
Another pumpkin waits to take my place.
It's an evil cycle.
Another pumpkin with frightening eyes and an evil smile.

Talking Tree

Talking tree,
Talking tree.
You speak words so gently.

You have great knowledge.
When Mother Nature comes,
You bow your head with homage.

You know so much of the past.
When you tell a story,
it comes to life.

The stories you tell,
Come from long ago.
I rest my head on the grass of your meadow.

Your voice sends me to my rest.
I dream about what you have said.

I will come again tomorrow,
Talking tree.
I like to listen to you and your rustling leaves.

It gives me peace,
From my busy world.
You I cherish like a Pot of Gold.

Beautiful Angel

Beautiful angel,
Please don't cry.
Save your tears for the good when they die.

Beautiful angel,
With a soul created by the light.
You never sleep,
You are my protector through the night.

Watch over me,
Gentle angel.
As I fall into a deep sleep.
You kiss me good night,
But your soul still weeps.

Lady of the Mist

Lady of the mist.
You have a gentle spirit.
Nature loves and cherishes your wanting wish.

To find a love for your heart.
Only in death your love shall depart.

You live always in a dream.
The flowers in your hair,
Sway to Nature's breeze.

When you touch a tree,
You know the sadness within.
Pillars of wood,
They hold up the sky.
So life can be alive and strong.
Your gift of your love is worthy of a song.

Golden Brown

Leaves dancing upon the wind.
Where it takes them is a dream.
The change of the season,
Kisses the trees goodnight.
They wake when the Summer lights up the celestial heights.

Patchwork of nature on the ground.
Leaves of golden brown.
Hides Nature's children from the wintry sky.
Nature's binds them to her love which will never die.

Every leaf holds the spirit of Autumn and the Summer gone.
They gave shade to the birds of air,
From the mid-day sun.

The Winter of November

Never,
Ever to forget.
Always to remember,
The Winter of November.

Lost,
To her Mother.
A child,
A baby girl.
Without shelter.

Not even a stable to call her home.
Lost to the Winter of yesterday.
Hoping for a new better tomorrow,
To come her way.

Sadness makes a home within and remains.
As her silent,
Unseen friend.

The Spirit

I stand and listen to the wind.
it is the spirit of everything.
It speaks to me.
My innocence has given it a voice.
When it speaks,
I just find within it joy.
Never to be alone.
My friend the wind,
Will always be with me till my life's end.

To follow a Star

Oh, spirit.
You entered my dreams.
I heard your voice across the darkness of belief.

Your message,
My soul welcomed with joy.
You wish us to take a journey and see a baby boy.

What we have seen written in the stars.
Have come true.
We are the chosen few.
To witness the Lord of the Word.
His spirit will save our world.

An Angels Tears

An angel with tears.
Father Time watched over her for many years.

Touched by the thorn of sadness,
From the crown of Our Lord.
She takes upon herself the sadness and pain of this world.

The purest of heart.
Her road is so long.
To make His pain her own.
She cries all alone.

God in heaven wishes to send her an ending.
But she only wishes her road is only her beginning.

To Wake from a Dream

To wake from a dream.
To wake from perfection.
I found myself in heaven.

A kingdom of glory.
A kingdom from a biblical story.
Enchantment and beauty lived there.
The realm of perfect peace dwelled there.

A place I long to return.
The memory of this dream,
Will take me through the day is long.

Sad Clown

The sad clown is always sad.
When he is around children,
They wish to make him glad.

Every tear he sheds,
Leaves its mark.
The children wish him to laugh.

The sad clown,
Cries alone.
He has lost the gift of happiness.
Now, he only knows the shadow of sadness.

The children hold the key.
Inside the Clown holds so much misery.
But how can the children bring him joy.
Their gift of play,
Will make him happy this day.

He watches the children.
One touches his painted tear.
With this his tear disappears.

This child is a golden light.
He is Jesus.
He gives happiness,
Where there was no life.

Naughty Gnome

I know of a naughty gnome,
Who doesn't conform.
He breaks every rule under the mid-day sun.

The other gnomes are frightened by him.
As they bring the joy of the day in.

The naughty gnome loves being very naughty.
He plays tricks on every body.

He ponders what he is going to do,
As he sits on his mushroom.

Being naughty fills his day and makes him happy.
The naughty gnome enjoys being very, very naughty.

This naughty gnome is a menace to society.
He will still be naughty,
When he is a hundred and ninety.

But at the end of the day,
He is only doing what comes naturally.

Reginald the Rat

Reginald the rat,
Wears a top hat.
He doesn't live down a drain.
He lives down the lane.
He lives in Mayfair.
He loves it there.

Reginald enjoys Champagne and caviar.
He sometimes swings on the chandelier.

His best time of the day.
Is when he reads the Financial Times and checks his watch when the Grand Father clock chimes.

Bundle of Joy

My puppy is a Golden Retriever.
He enjoys licking my face all over.
I give him treats.
As he is my good boy.
He is my bundle of joy.

He runs around all day long.
Carrying his favourite toy,
Which is a log.

When he bites it,
It squeaks.
He enjoys taking it back to his bed when it is his time to sleep.

Lightning Source UK Ltd.
Milton Keynes UK
UKHW051041181120
373595UK00002B/37